Katy Duck

and the Secret Valentine

By Alyssa Satin Capucilli   Illustrated by Henry Cole

Ready-to-Read

Simon Spotlight

New York   London   Toronto   Sydney   New Delhi

For Jordan Lilly, Bryce Meyer, and
Oliver Parker—my newest valentines!
—A. S. C.

For QK . . . my secret valentine!
—H. C.

SIMON SPOTLIGHT
An imprint of Simon & Schuster Children's Publishing Division
1230 Avenue of the Americas, New York, New York 10020
First Simon Spotlight edition December 2014
Text copyright © 2014 by Alyssa Satin Capucilli
Illustrations copyright © 2014 by Henry Cole
For information about special discounts for bulk purchases, please contact
Simon & Schuster Special Sales at 1-866-506-1949 or business@simonandschuster.com.
The Simon & Schuster Speakers Bureau can bring authors to your live event.
For more information or to book an event contact the Simon & Schuster Speakers Bureau at
1-866-248-3049 or visit our website at www.simonspeakers.com.
Manufactured in the United States of America 1114 LAK
10 9 8 7 6 5 4 3 2 1
Library of Congress Cataloging-in-Publication Data
Capucilli, Alyssa Satin, 1957– author.
Katy Duck and the secret valentine / by Alyssa Satin Capucilli ;
illustrated by Henry Cole. — First edition.
pages cm — (Ready-to-read. Level 1)
Summary: "When Katy Duck receives a secret valentine filled with sparkly stars, she wonders who
it could be from! With a little help from her friend Ralph, Katy makes the perfect card for her secret
valentine . . . and discovers who it is!"— Provided by publisher.
ISBN 978-1-4424-9809-9 (paperback) — ISBN 978-1-4424-9810-5 (hc) — ISBN 978-1-4424-9811-2
(ebook) [1. Valentines—Fiction. 2. Friendship—Fiction. 3. Ducks—Fiction.] I. Cole, Henry, 1955-
illustrator. II. Title.
PZ7.C179Kae 2014
[E]—dc23
2014024376

It was Valentine's Day.
The mailman had a special
delivery for Katy Duck!

Katy was excited.

"Tra-la-la. Quack! Quack!"

She leaped and twirled.

Then she opened the card.
It was filled with
hearts and flowers.

There were lots of
sparkly stars.
And lots of glue, too.

Roses are red,
violets are blue,
I am glad to have a
friend like you!
Guess who?

"Tra-la-la. Guess who?"
said Katy Duck.

"Who could my
secret valentine be?"

Just then the doorbell rang.

It was Ralph.

"Zip—zoom—whoosh!"
said Ralph.
"Let us play!"

"Tra-la-la. Quack! Quack!
I cannot play now, Ralph,"
said Katy Duck.

"I have a secret valentine.
I must make a card
right away!"

"Tra-la-la. But wait!"
said Katy Duck.
"I do not know what my
secret valentine likes."

Katy fluttered her arms.
"Does my valentine
like swans?" she asked.

"Or race cars?" said Ralph.

Katy flew here and there.

"Maybe my valentine likes butterflies."

"Or airplanes," said Ralph.

"Zip—zoom—whoosh!
Or rocket ships," he said.
"Blast off!"

"That is a great idea,
Ralph," said Katy Duck.
"Will you help me
make a card?"

Ralph helped Katy
draw a rocket ship.
He made lots of
sparkly stars, too.

"Hey, Ralph," said Katy.
"You made sparkly stars just
like my secret valentine did!"

Now Ralph smiled.
"Are you my secret
valentine?" asked Katy Duck.
Ralph nodded.

Katy Duck

leaped.

She twirled.

"Roses are red,
violets are blue,
I am glad to have a friend
like you too, Ralph,"
said Katy.

"Tra-la-la. Quack! Quack!
Happy Valentine's Day.
Now we can play!"